The Magic Key

The Demon Drill

OXFORD
UNIVERSITY PRESS

Nadim was putting up a display of drills in his family's shop window. The gang tried to help but Nadim wanted to do it all by himself. He'd been waiting ages for the Demon Drills to arrive, and was even wearing his Demon Drill T-shirt.

'We could put some other tools in the window as well,' suggested Biff. 'Like these pliers!'

'No, Biff,' said Nadim, snatching the pliers away from her. 'This is a drills-only display!'

He added one last drill, and went outside to admire his display.

But it began to wobble. √ A R √

And then it fell down. CRASH! Boxes flew everywhere.

'Why won't you let me help?' cried Biff.

I wish he'd let *me* help, thought Floppy. People need to see the dog food!

Just then, the key on Floppy's collar started to glow.

Suddenly, Biff, Nadim, and Floppy were dragged into a vortex of amazing colours and lights. They were flying round and round, faster and faster . . .

Biff, Nadim, and Floppy looked around. They could see a half-built boat – and a big drill waving at them from the deck. He pointed to Nadim's T-shirt.

'I see you're a Demon Drill!' he said, hopping out of the boat. 'We could really do with you below deck.'

Nadim liked the idea of helping to build the boat, and agreed to go.

Then the drill, whose name was Danny, looked at Biff.

'What's a pair of pliers doing here?' he asked. ' And you must be a sander by the look of you,' he added, pointing to Floppy.

Biff and Floppy stared at him, feeling very confused.

'It's drills only around here,' Danny went on. 'Demon Drill – you come with me.'

Nadim went off with Danny, so Biff and Floppy decided to explore. At the quayside they soon met three screwdrivers. But when Biff tried to talk to them, they ignored her!

The same thing happened a little further on, when Biff and Floppy met a group of saws.

'We don't talk to pliers!' one of them snapped at her.

Meanwhile, Danny showed Nadim around the boat. Two drills were trying to cut the mast to size by drilling holes in it. It was taking them a very long time.

'Er – wouldn't a saw do that quicker?' Nadim asked.

'Saw?' squeaked one of the drills. 'We don't work with saws. We're drills!'

Back on the quayside, Biff and Floppy had met some friendly pliers who were warming themselves up round a fire. They asked Biff if she would like a cup of tea.

'Yes, please,' she replied. She began to talk to the pliers, so Floppy went off for a sniff around.

'There's no work around here, I'm afraid,' one pair of pliers told her sadly.

'The drills took this job,' another explained.

The third pair of pliers explained that to finish the job, the drills had to launch the boat that day. 'And now they'll get the prize,' he added wistfully, pointing at a huge toolbox.

It looked like a little house, and the door had a red ribbon tied round the handle, like a present. Biff looked at it thoughtfully. Then she realized that Floppy was nowhere to be seen.

'Excuse me, I think I should find my dog,' she said, putting down her cup.

Inside the boat, Nadim looked in confusion at two drills that were working on the floorboards. Then he had an idea.

'You need a screwdriver!' Nadim said. 'I'll see if I can find one.'

The drills stared after him as he raced off.

'Why does he think we need a screwdriver?' muttered one.

'If you ask me, that Demon Drill's a bit too big for his boots,' said the other.

Nadim quickly found the group of screwdrivers at the quayside.

'We need a screwdriver on board,' he said.

'What a cheek!' said one.

'We said all along it was a job for screwdrivers, not drills,' the second one agreed.

And the three of them rudely turned their backs on him.

Nadim sighed. But then he noticed the saws and went up to them.
'We desperately need a saw to cut the mast to size,' he told them.
But the three saws just ignored him.
'Why are you all being so rude?' Nadim wailed.
'Rude?' one of the saws snorted. 'You drills grabbed the job in the first place. You sort it out!'

Nadim felt confused. Why wouldn't the tools work together? Just then, he saw Biff and Floppy.

'Am I glad I found you!' he said. 'You've got to help me! The drills are about to launch the boat, but it's not finished. It'll sink!'

Nadim, Biff, and Floppy ran back to the boat. Danny Drill was just about to launch it.

'Stop!' Nadim yelled. 'You can't launch the boat. It's full of holes!'

Danny looked annoyed. 'Of course it's full of holes!' he said. 'We're drills, aren't we? We're launching now, or we won't get the prize.'

Nadim turned to all the other drills. 'This is too dangerous,' he told them. 'We've GOT to ask the other tools to help.'

He turned towards the quayside. 'Calling all tools!' he shouted. 'Any tool that comes to help build this boat will get a share of the prize. But you ALL have to come NOW!'

Soon, lots of tools began to help. Danny was furious.

'I'm in charge of this boat!' he yelled. 'What do you think you're doing, Demon?'

Nadim ignored him. 'Below deck, please, double quick,' he told the screwdrivers.

'Now we'll have to share the prize with all the other tools!' said Danny.

'The only way to get the job done is to work together,' Nadim told him.

Danny went quiet. Then he looked around at all the work that was being done, and at last a smile broke over his face.

'Nice one, Demon!' he said. 'I wonder why we never thought of working together before?'

It wasn't long before the boat was finished – and sailing beautifully!

'Well done, all you tools,' Nadim said. 'By working together, you did a great job. You've really earned your prize.'

The tools cheered as Nadim undid the ribbon around the toolbox, and put it in his pocket.

'A tool store for ALL us tools to share!' Danny smiled.

Just then, Biff noticed Floppy's collar. 'The key's glowing!' she said. We're going! thought Floppy.

Back at the Shah's shop, Wilf, Wilma, Chip, and Kipper saw that Nadim was removing the drills from the window display. They pushed the shop door open.

'It looks like Nadim's changed his mind,' Wilma said.

He certainly had! 'Biff and I are making a display of ALL the tools,' Nadim said.

Biff was busy writing something on a big piece of card, and when she'd finished, Nadim took the ribbon from his pocket, and stuck it onto the card.

The poster was complete.

'Shah's sells a tool for every job!' read Biff, and she winked at Nadim. 'Nice one, Demon!'

OXFORD
UNIVERSITY PRESS

Great Clarendon Street, Oxford OX2 6DP

Oxford University Press is a department of the University of Oxford.
It furthers the University's objective of excellence in research, scholarship,
and education by publishing worldwide in

Oxford New York

Auckland Cape Town Dar es Salaam Hong Kong Karachi
Kuala Lumpur Madrid Melbourne Mexico City Nairobi
New Delhi Shanghai Taipei Toronto

With offices in

Argentina Austria Brazil Chile Czech Republic France Greece
Guatemala Hungary Italy Japan Poland Portugal Singapore
South Korea Switzerland Thailand Turkey Ukraine Vietnam

Oxford is a registered trade mark of Oxford University Press in the UK and in certain other countries

British Library Cataloguing in Publication Data available
ISBN-13: 978-019-272651-3
ISBN-10: 0-19-272651-X
3 5 7 9 10 8 6 4 2
Printed in China